Is This You?

By RUTH KRAUSS and CROCKETT JOHNSON

SCHOLASTIC INC.

New York Toronto London Auckland Sydney

Is this your family?

ISBN 0-590-41196-9

Text copyright ©1955 by Ruth Krauss.
Drawings copyright ©1955 by Crockett Johnson
This book was originally published by William R. Scott, Inc.

15 16 17 18   08   9/0

Printed in the U.S.A.

Is this your family?

Is this?

Is this your family?

This?

Get some pages of paper
all the same size
and draw your family
on one of them.

Is this where you live?

Is this where?

Is this?

Is this where you live?

Is this where?

Take another page
of your paper and draw
where you live.

Is this what you eat for breakfast?

Is this what?

Is this?

This?

This?

Take another page of
your paper and draw what
you eat for breakfast.

This makes three pages.

Is this your name?

Is this?

This?

Is this your name?

This?

Is this?

Now take another page
of your paper
and write your name.

This makes page four.

Is this where you go to school?

Is this where?

Is this?

Is this where you go to school?

Is this?

Page five — draw where
you go to school.

Is this your friend?

Is this?

Is this?

Is this your friend?

This?

Page six — draw your friend.

Is this what you want for your birthday?

Is this what you want for your birthday?

Is this what?

Is this?

Page seven — draw what you
want for your birthday.

Is this how you go places?

Is this how?

Is this how?

Is this?

Is this how you go places?

Is this how?

Page eight — draw how you go places.

Is this how you take a bath?

Is this how?

Is this how?

Is this?

Page nine — draw how
you take a bath.

Is this your bed?

Is this?

VEGETABLES

Is this your bed?

This?

Page ten — draw your bed.

Is this you?

Is this you?

Is this?

This?

This?

Is this you?

Is this?

This?

Page eleven — draw yourself.

Now take two more pages of your paper.
Put all your drawings between them,
and you have a book with covers.

Staple or sew the book together
on the left-hand side.